MYSTERY MACHINE SPOOK

By Michelle H. Nagler
Illustrated by Duendes del Sur

ABDOPUBLISHING.COM

Reinforced library bound edition published in 2017 by Spotlight, a division of ABDO. PO Box 398166, Minneapolis, Minnesota 55439. Spotlight produces high-quality reinforced library bound editions for schools and libraries. Published by agreement with Warner Bros. Entertainment Inc.

Printed in the United States of America, North Mankato, Minnesota.
042016   092016

THIS BOOK CONTAINS
RECYCLED MATERIALS

PUBLISHER'S CATALOGING IN PUBLICATION DATA

Names: Nagler, Michelle H., author. | Duendes del Sur, illustrator.
Title: Scooby-Doo and the mystery machine spook / by Michelle H. Nagler ; illustrated by Duendes del Sur.
Description: Minneapolis, MN : Spotlight, [2017] | Series: Scooby-Doo early reading adventures
Summary: Scooby and the gang are decorating the mystery machine for a parade. But when someone or something messes up their hard work, it's up to the gang to solve the mystery and fix the mystery machine in time for the big parade.
Identifiers: LCCN 2016930651 | ISBN 9781614794707 (lib. bdg.)
Subjects: LCSH: Scooby-Doo (Fictitious character)--Juvenile fiction. | Dogs--Juvenile fiction. | Parades--Juvenile fiction. | Mystery and detective stories--Juvenile fiction. | Adventure and adventurers--Juvenile fiction.
Classification: DDC [Fic]--dc23
LC record available at http://lccn.loc.gov/2016930651

Spotlight
A Division of ABDO
abdopublishing.com

Scooby and the gang were
decorating the Mystery Machine
for a parade.

Velma and Daphne hung colorful
paper, streamers and balloons.
Scooby added some paint.

"We're going to win a trophy!"
Fred said.

"Like, let's get some grub first,"
said Shaggy.

Fred locked the Mystery Machine
in the garage and the gang left to
eat dinner.

The next day, they returned to the garage and were shocked at what they found.

The Mystery Machine was not as they had left it.

The paper and streamers were crumpled on the floor.

The balloons were deflated and the paint was spilled.

"Who would wreck our Mystery Machine?" Velma asked.

"Maybe it was a ghost," Shaggy said.

"Let's split up and look for clues," said Fred. "Daphne, Velma and I will look outside. Scooby and Shaggy, you search the garage."

Scooby and Shaggy looked at the torn paper, streamers and balloons.

Scooby saw something moving under the paper.

"Rook!" pointed Scooby.

"Zoinks!" cried Shaggy.

The object squeaked.

It was only a mouse.

Then Scooby saw a big, scary shadow behind the Mystery Machine.

"Maybe it's the ghost!" Shaggy said.

Scooby jumped into Shaggy's arms.

But it was only a pile of paint cans.

"Like, let's look for clues someplace else," Shaggy said.

"Rokay!" said Scooby.

Scooby and Shaggy left the garage and went outside.

The parade was getting ready to start.

"Let's check the food stand for clues," Shaggy said.

The man selling ice cream did not have any clues for them.

But he did have lots of ice cream.

Scooby and Shaggy saw Velma talking to a boy and girl from the band.

"I heard howling in the garage," said the girl. "I looked through the window and saw your Mystery Machine."

"Did you see a ghost?" asked Shaggy.

"No," said the girl.

"I saw flashes of light," said the boy.

The band went to line up for the parade.

"We have to fix the Mystery Machine," said Velma. "It's almost time for the parade."

"Scooby, will you and Shaggy get a head start?" asked Fred.

Scooby shook his head no.

"Like, there's a ghost!" said Shaggy.

"Would you do it for a Scooby-Snack?" asked Daphne.

"Rokay!" Scooby barked.

Scooby and Shaggy went back
to the garage.

The door was locked so Scooby
climbed in through the window.

They cleaned up the spilled
paint, torn paper and streamers.

Then they heard a noise.

"Uh-oh," said Shaggy.

"Rhost!" said Scooby.

But it was only Fred, Daphne
and Velma!

"How did you get in?" asked
Shaggy.

"We forgot to give you the key,"
Fred said.

"How did you get in?" Velma
asked.

"The window," Shaggy said.

"Hmm," said Velma. "I think I
have this mystery solved."

"There was a storm last night," Velma said. "We forgot to close the window when we left the garage. The wind and rain came in and ripped the paper, streamers and balloons off the Mystery Machine."

"And it spilled the paint," Shaggy said.

"Right!" said Velma. "The wind made the howling noise and the flashing light was lightning."

"Looks like we've got this mystery solved," said Fred. "Now let's get ready for the parade!"

Scooby and the gang
redecorated the Mystery
Machine in time for the parade.
And they won a first place
trophy.

"Scooby, we couldn't have done
it without you!" Velma said.

"Scooby-Dooby-Doo!" barked
Scooby.

The End